WHAT **IS** IT THAT MAKES US WHAT WE **ARE**?

IS IT OUR SCHOOLING?

OR IS IT OUR **FAMILY**?

ALEX RIDER.

FAMILY. HAVE YOU **PREPARED** SOMETHING FOR US?

OH! UM... YES.

COME ON, THEN.

GO ON.

YEAH.

OK.

I DIDN'T EVEN **KNOW** MY PARENTS. THEY **DIED** WHEN I WAS SMALL. I LIVE WITH MY **UNCLE**, AND HE'S NOT THERE MUCH **EITHER**.

THERE'S NOT MUCH I CAN **SAY** ABOUT MY FAMILY.

I HAVE A SORT OF HOUSEKEEPER INSTEAD, BECAUSE HE'S ALWAYS AWAY ON **BUSINESS**.

CORNWALL

"HE'S GOT A REALLY **BORING** JOB."

"HE'S A **BANK SUPERVISOR**. HE'S IN CHARGE OF **CUSTOMER CARE**."

BOOM!

BRAKKA

"YOU KNOW..."

PORT TALLON
Welcomes
Careful Drivers

"...LIFE IN THE *SLOW LANE.*"

VRRRRM!

RI D3R

"I WOULDN'T SAY *I* WAS MUCH LIKE HIM..."

BEETHOVEN
DISC 3   02:56

BEEP

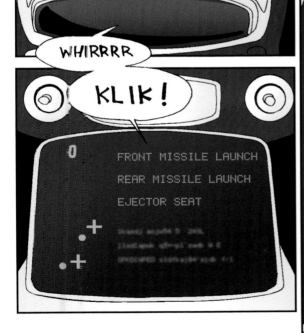

WHIRRRR

KLIK!

0
FRONT MISSILE LAUNCH
REAR MISSILE LAUNCH
EJECTOR SEAT

0   FRONT MIS

TARGET
LOCKED   REA   MISS

DIT

DIT

DIIIIIIIII...

HEY, SABINA.

OH...

HI, ALEX.

I WAS *WONDERING*... DO YOU WANT TO *DO* SOMETHING THIS WEEKEND?

NO.

I MEAN, *I CAN'T.*

I HAVE *RIDING LESSONS* ON SATURDAY, AND THEN I'M GOING *OUT* WITH MY MUM AND DAD.

OH!

SORRY...

IT DOESN'T MATTER.

MAYBE *NEXT* WEEKEND!

WHATEVER.

BEEP BEEP

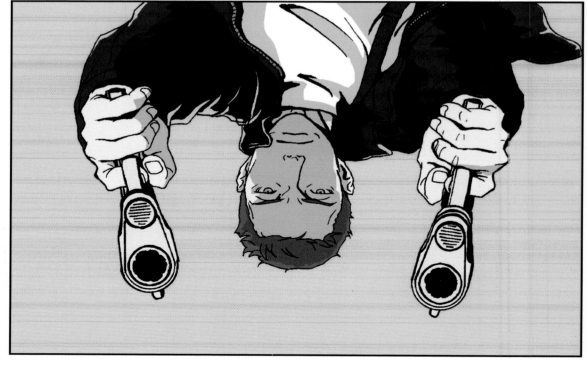

ALEX RIDER

ACTION
ADRENALINE
ADVENTURE

STORMBREAKER

THE GRAPHIC NOVEL

WALKER

ANTHONY HOROWITZ

ANTONY JOHNSTON • KANAKO • YUZURU

First published 2006 by Walker Books Ltd
87 Vauxhall Walk, London SE11 5HJ

This edition published 2016

2 4 6 8 10 9 7 5 3

Text and illustrations © 2006 Walker Books Ltd
Based on the original novel *Stormbreaker* © 2000 Stormbreaker Productions Ltd
Screenplay © MMVI Samuelsons / IoM Film
Film © MMVI Film and Entertainment
VIP Medienfonds 4 GmbH & Co. KG and UK Film Council
Style Guide © MMVI ARR Ltd

Anthony Horowitz has asserted his moral rights.

Trademarks © 2006 Stormbreaker Productions Ltd
Stormbreaker™, Alex Rider™, Boy with Torch Logo™, AR Logo™

This book has been typeset in Wild Words and Serpentine Bold

Printed in China

British Library Cataloguing in Publication data:
a catalogue record for this book is available from the British Library

ISBN 978-1-4063-6632-7

www.walker.co.uk

PATRIOT?

FORASMUCH AS IT HATH **PLEASED** ALMIGHTY GOD, OF HIS GREAT **MERCY**...

WHIRR...

...TO TAKE **UNTO** HIMSELF THE SOUL OF OUR DEAR BROTHER HERE **DEPARTED**...

...WE THEREFORE COMMIT HIS BODY TO THE *GROUND*, IN *SURE AND CERTAIN HOPE* OF THE RESURRECTION TO *ETERNAL LIFE*.

AMEN.

COME ON, LET'S JUST GO *HOME*.

ALEX?

MY NAME IS *JOHN CRAWFORD*.

I'M WITH THE *ROYAL & GENERAL BANK*, AND I WANT YOU TO KNOW YOU HAVE ALL OUR CONDOLENCES.

IT'S AN ABSOLUTE *TRAGEDY*. A *CAR ACCIDENT*! IF ONLY HE'D BEEN WEARING A *SEAT BELT*...

THANK YOU—

THIS IS *ALAN BLUNT*, THE BANK *CHAIRMAN*.

HE'D LIKE A WORD.

I'M **VERY** SORRY ABOUT YOUR UNCLE, ALEX. WE'RE GOING TO **MISS** HIM.

HE TALKED A **LOT** ABOUT YOU.

THAT'S STRANGE... BECAUSE HE **NEVER** MENTIONED YOU.

THIS IS MY DEPUTY, **MRS JONES**.

I'LL BE IN **CONTACT** WITH YOU VERY **SOON**, ALEX.

WHY?

ERM, **WELL**...

AFTER WHAT'S **HAPPENED**. THERE'S THE QUESTION OF WHO WILL LOOK **AFTER** YOU...

I'LL LOOK AFTER HIM.

WE JUST WANT TO **HELP**...

NOT CAREFUL **ENOUGH**.

I'M **SURE** WE'LL MEET **AGAIN**, ALEX. HOPEFULLY SOMEWHERE A LITTLE LESS... **GLOOMY**.

MY UNCLE **ALWAYS** WORE HIS **SEATBELT**, MR BLUNT.

HE WAS A VERY **CAREFUL** MAN.

DID YOU **MEAN** WHAT YOU **SAID**? ABOUT LOOKING **AFTER** ME?

OF **COURSE** I DID! COME ON, YOU **KNOW** I WOULDN'T LEAVE YOU. ANYWAY, WHO **ELSE** IS THERE?

BUT WILL YOU BE **ALLOWED** TO? I MEAN, WE'RE NOT EVEN **RELATED**.

I'VE BEEN **LIVING** WITH YOU FOR **NINE YEARS**. HOW MUCH **MORE** RELATED DO YOU WANT TO BE?

WAS IT JUST **ME**, OR WAS THERE SOMETHING ABOUT THOSE **BANKERS** THAT STRUCK YOU AS **WEIRD**?

JACK...!

!

HEY THAT'S ALL **IAN'S** STUFF! WHAT ARE YOU **DOING**?

HEY!

BRooooo....

JEFF SLATER
AUTO WRECKERS
HEAVEN FOR CARS

SOUTH LONDON

HEY!

YOU SEEN *NIGEL*?

NAH.

WELL, IF YOU *SEE* HIM, TELL HIM I *WANT* HIM.

BRAKKA

BRAKKA BRAKKA

BRAKKA

HEY—

EURGH!

I COULDN'T BELIEVE WHAT I WAS *DOING*. THIS GUY JUST CAME *AT ME*, AND...

WHAT WERE *THEY*...
OW!

...DOING, JACK? AND WHY WERE THEY *HERE*?

COME *UPSTAIRS* AND SEE FOR *YOURSELF*...

CHELSEA

WHO THE **HELL** DO YOU THINK **YOU** ARE? A **SCHOOLBOY!**

WHAT'S YOUR **NAME?** WHO **SENT** YOU HERE?

I CAN'T TELL YOU.

OH, YOU CAN TELL **ME.**

NO...

YOU WITH **SPECIAL OPERATIONS?** THEY'RE THE ONLY ONES **DAFT** ENOUGH TO COME UP WITH SOMETHING LIKE THIS.

I ... SAID ...

...I CAN'T **TELL** YOU!

SOMEONE BEEN TEACHING YOU **SELF-DEFENCE,** EH? WELL, **THAT** WON'T HELP YOU HERE.

YOU WON'T LAST **TWO DAYS.**

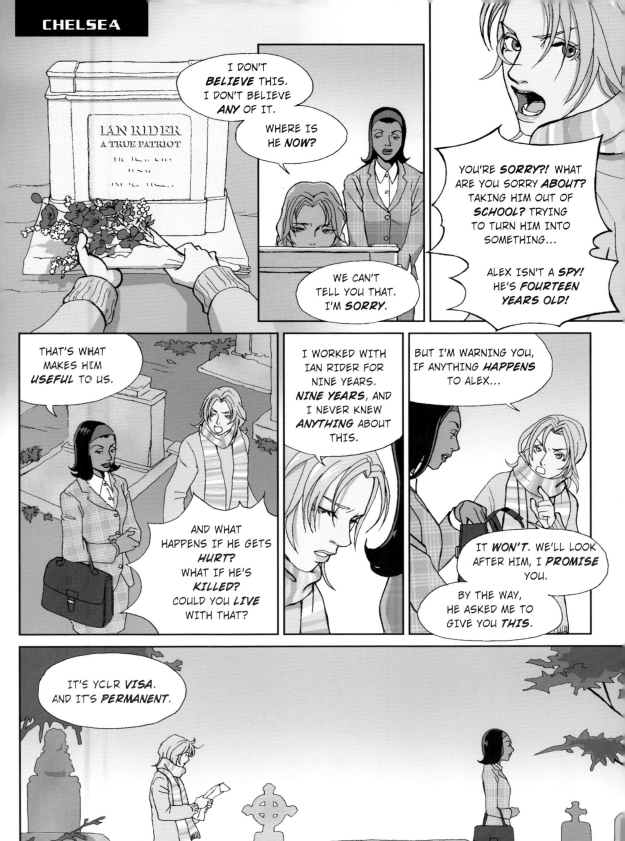

HFF

HFF

KEEP THAT GUN ABOVE YOUR HEAD...

GEBL RGBR LRGR GLBR GR GLLBRGR!

BRECON BEACONS

YOU'RE NOT IN THE *PLAYGROUND* NOW, CUB! *MOVE IT!*

LET ME GIVE YOU A *HAND*, CUB.

NO, *WAI...T!*

AAAAAAAAH

BLOOP!

HAHAHA!

HAHAHA HAHA!

HAHAHAHA!

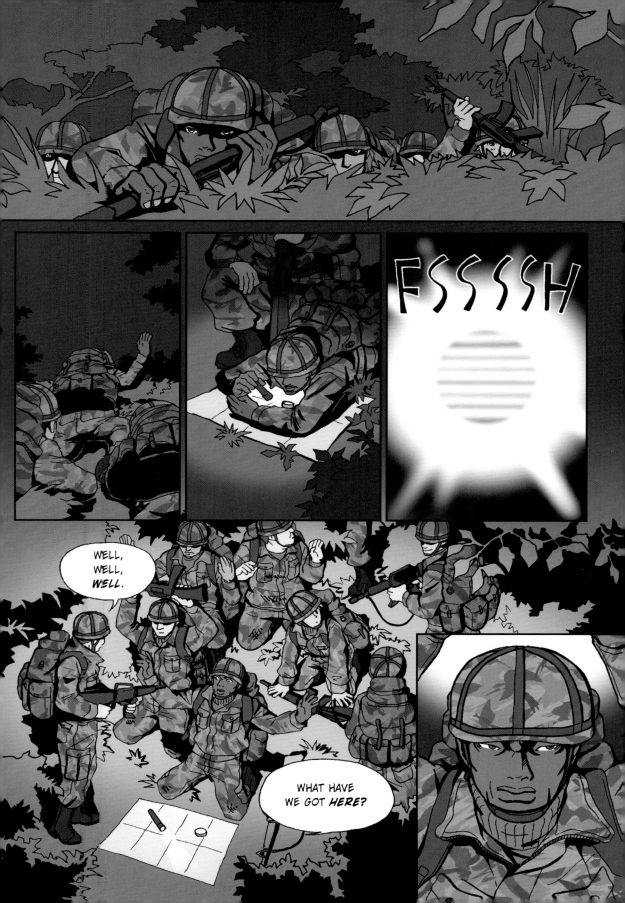

KIYAAAI!

KRASH

THERE'S A *FIREPLACE*.

HOW DID *YOU* KNOW?

I SAW THE *CHIMNEY* ON THE WAY IN.

THE KID'S RIGHT. IT'S *CLEAR*.

YEAH, *RIGHT*. YOU THINK THEY'D JUST *LEAVE* IT IF THEY THOUGHT WE COULD ALL CLIMB *UP?*

YOU CAN'T. YOU'RE TOO BIG.

ANYTHING HAPPENING?

NAH.

BUNCH OF *LOSERS*.

WHY'D THEY HAVE A *KID* WITH THEM?

I DON'T KNOW...

MMMPH!

BIT *YOUNG* FOR THE SPECIAL FORCES.

BOSS...

YEAH? WHAT *IS* IT?

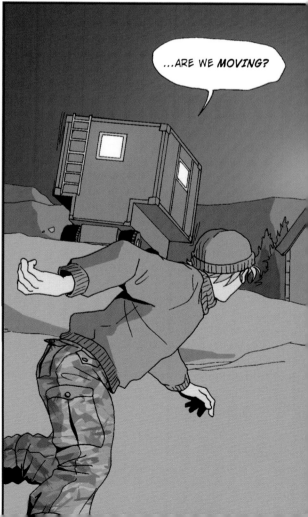

...ARE WE *MOVING*?

SPLOSH!

CUTS, BRUISES, FRACTURED LIMBS...

IT'S A MIRACLE NO ONE WAS **KILLED!**

HE'S NOT A **CHILD**, HE'S A **LETHAL WEAPON.**

I'M **VERY** SORRY, MAJOR. WE WILL BE **TALKING** TO OUR MAN.

SORRY, **BOY.**

HE'S READY.

AND FINALLY,

THE MOST **GENEROUS** GIFT **EVER MADE** TO THE BRITISH NATION.

THE **STORMBREAKER** HAS BEEN CALLED THE MOST **SOPHISTICATED** PERSONAL COMPUTER OF THE 21ST CENTURY...

HEADLINES: EVERY SCHOOL IN THE UK TO BE GIVEN THE STORMBREAKER... ...EST

...AND LAST MONTH, ITS MULTIBILLIONAIRE INVENTOR, **DARRIUS SAYLE**, MADE HIS ASTONISHING **ANNOUNCEMENT**.

LIVE

THAT'S **RIGHT**, VIVIEN. I WANT TO GIVE A **FREE STORMBREAKER** TO **EVERY** SCHOOL IN THE COUNTRY.

PHISTICATED PC.

AND WHILE I'M **AT** IT, I WOULDN'T MIND GIVING **YOU** ONE TOO.

LIVE

REALLY, MR SAYLE!

PC. DARRIUS SAYLE S... ...ONTRIBUT

THE **PRIME MINISTER** HAS GIVEN HIS FULL SUPPORT...

THIS IS A **WONDERFUL** OPPORTUNITY FOR BRITISH SCHOOLS, AND I'M **HONOURED** THAT MR SAYLE HAS ASKED **ME** TO PRESS THE BUTTON THAT WILL BRING ALL THE COMPUTERS **ON-LINE**.

'OOL IN THE UK TO BE GIVEN THE STORMBREAKER.

...JUST AS IT HAS **RECENTLY** COME TO LIGHT THAT HE AND MR SAYLE WERE AT **SCHOOL** TOGETHER.

FORTUNE

Inside
Darrius Sayle
....
....
....

THE EDUCATION SYSTEM. THE STORMBREAKER IS TH

FORTU
Inside
Darrius Sayle

WE DON'T **TRUST** HIM.

WHY NOT?

WELL, WE DON'T TRUST **ANYONE**. IT'S SORT OF WHAT WE'RE **FOR**.

KLIK

WE ALWAYS **THOUGHT** DARRIUS SAYLE WAS TOO **GOOD** TO BE **TRUE**. SO, SIX MONTHS AGO, WE SENT AN AGENT TO KEEP AN **EYE** ON HIM.

YOU MEAN MY **UNCLE**.

YES.

SAYLE HAS A **MANUFACTURING PLANT** IN **CORNWALL**, BUILT ON TOP OF WHAT USED TO BE A **TIN MINE**. IAN RIDER WENT THERE AS A **SECURITY GUARD**...

...AND HE **FOUND** SOMETHING. IN HIS LAST MESSAGE TO US, HE MENTIONED A **VIRUS**.

A **COMPUTER VIRUS**...?

WE DON'T KNOW. HE WAS ON HIS WAY TO **TELL** US, BUT HE NEVER ARRIVED.

SOMETHING'S GOING ON. WE NEED TO GET SOMEONE **IN** THERE TO TAKE A LOOK **AROUND**.

AND THIS MAY BE OUR **LAST CHANCE**.

WHY **ME?**

THIS IS **KEVIN BLAKE**, A COMPUTER NERD. SIX WEEKS AGO HE WON A **COMPETITION** IN THIS MAGAZINE.

EVER **READ** IT?

...

THE **FIRST PRIZE** WAS A **VISIT** TO CORNWALL AND A CHANCE TO TRY OUT THE **STORMBREAKER**.

HE'S DUE TO ARRIVE **TOMORROW**.

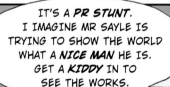

I'LL SHOW YOU.

IT'S A **PR STUNT**. I IMAGINE MR SAYLE IS TRYING TO SHOW THE WORLD WHAT A **NICE MAN** HE IS. GET A **KIDDY** IN TO SEE THE WORKS.

YOU'LL TAKE KEVIN'S PLACE.

BUT I'M NOTHING **LIKE** HIM.

WE'VE SPOKEN TO THE **EDITOR**.

!!

THERE'S JUST ONE **PROBLEM**...

I DON'T KNOW ANYTHING **ABOUT** COMPUTERS. I'M **NOT** A NERD.

BUT YOU SOON **WILL** BE.

WE ONLY HAVE **THREE DAYS** LEFT. THERE'S A LAUNCH AT **THE SCIENCE MUSEUM** NEXT FRIDAY. **70,000** STORMBREAKER COMPUTERS GOING LIVE...

...

WE **DON'T** WANT YOU TO GET INTO ANY **TROUBLE**, ALEX. JUST TAKE A LOOK **AROUND.** AND BE CAREFUL OF SAYLE. HE MAY **SEEM** CHARMING...

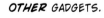

...BUT HE'S ABOUT AS CHARMING AS A **SNAKE**.

JUST KEEP YOUR **EYES** OPEN AND REPORT **BACK.**

BUT HOW WILL I DO **THAT**?

WE'LL SUPPLY YOU WITH A **TELECOMMUNICATIONS DEVICE**. THAT AND...

OTHER GADGETS.

I GET **GADGETS**?

EVENING NEWS

SAYLE LAUNCHES THE STORMBREAKER

IF YOU PAT HIS *HEAD*...

HIS *TAIL* WAGS.

HE ALSO OBEYS CERTAIN *VOICE* COMMANDS...

ROLL OVER!

KLUNK!

DELIGHTFUL, DON'T YOU THINK? WE ALSO HAVE ROBOT *CATS* AND *RODENTS*—

EXCUSE ME.

I'M LOOKING FOR SOMETHING TO TAKE TO *CORNWALL*.

GEEE

GEEEE

AH.

CORNWALL, YES.

COME WITH ME...

GEE GEEE

FOUNTAIN PEN.

NOT USED BY MANY YOUNG PEOPLE THESE DAYS, ALAS...

THE **NIB** CAN BE FIRED FROM A RANGE OF SIX METRES, AND THE INK IS **SODIUM PENTATHOL**. WHOEVER YOU HIT WILL DO **EXACTLY** WHAT YOU TELL THEM FOR THE NEXT **SIX HOURS**.

BUT I'VE SAVED THE **BEST** 'TIL **LAST**...

A **MODIFIED NINTENDO DS**. WHAT IT DOES DEPENDS ON THE **CARTRIDGE** THAT YOU PLACE IN IT.

SLIP IN THIS GAME, **CALL-UP**, AND IT'S A **PDA SCANNER AND TRANSMITTER**. THAT'S HOW YOU KEEP IN **TOUCH** WITH US.

PANIC STATION IS A **BUG-FINDER AND SONIC INTENSIFIER**. YOU CAN HEAR A CONVERSATION **TWO ROOMS** AWAY.

THIS ONE IS CALLED **GREEN SCREEN**. IT TURNS THE WHOLE THING INTO A **SMOKE BOMB**, WITH A **FIVE SECOND** FUSE.

WHAT ABOUT **MARIO KART?**

OH, THAT'S JUST A **GAME**.

I THOUGHT YOU MIGHT LIKE IT FOR THE **FLIGHT**.

CHELSEA

IT'S FROM *CORNWALL!*

GREETINGS FROM CORNWALL

BUT HE DIDN'T MEAN YOU TO GO THERE *NOW*, ALEX. THAT'S NOT WHAT HE *MEANT...*

IT'S ONLY A FEW DAYS, JACK.

I'LL BE *CAREFUL.*

YOU REALLY *PROMISE* ME?

I *PROMISE.*

AND ALEX...

WHAT?

ANOTHER *GADGET?*

WHAT IS IT, A *LOCKPICK?* DOES IT *EXPLODE?*

NO, ALEX.

IT *CLEANS* YOUR *TEETH.*

KEVIN BLAKE!

MRS VOLE, IS THAT RIGHT? I'M THE EDITOR OF *DISC DRIVE WORLD*...

THEN THIS MUST BE *KEVIN*, JA?

THAT'S ME.

GUT. YOU SHOULD SAY *GOODBYE* NOW.

GOODBYE, KEVIN! I HOPE YOU FIND YOUR STAY VERY *INFORMATIVE!*

←ARRIVAL

CAR PARK→

I'M SURE IT *WILL* BE...

I AM *NADIA VOLE.* I WORK FOR *MR SAYLE* IN *PR.*

PUBLIC RELATIONS?

JA. THIS IS *PORT TALLON.* A *FISHING VILLAGE.*

NICE PLACE.

NOT IF YOU ARE *A FISH.*

PORT TALLON Welcomes Careful Drivers

TAKE CARE.
JACK. XXX

MR SAYLE IS ALREADY HERE.

HE WILL SEE YOU
IMMEDIATELY FOR LUNCH.

IT'S **NINETY-NINE PER CENT WATER**. IT HAS NO **BRAINS**, AND NO **ANUS**.

THE **MAN OF WAR** IS AN **OUTSIDER**.

IT'S **SILENT**, YET IT DEMANDS **RESPECT**. THOSE **TENTACLES** ARE COVERED IN **NEMATOCYSTS**... STINGING CELLS. IF YOU CAME INTO **CONTACT** WITH THEM, YOU'D DIE A VERY **MEMORABLE** DEATH.

...

I THINK I'M GOING TO **LIKE** YOU.

I'M TOO **YOUNG** TO DIE.

NO, NO, **NO**. I WOULLDN'T BELIEVE **THAT**.

YOU'RE **NEVER** TOO YOUNG TO DIE.

WHAT THE...?

HIYA, CUDDLES.

MR SAYLE, THE **AMERICAN AMBASSADOR** IS ON LINE ONE.

FZZZZZZzzz

IT SEEMS I'M **NOT** GOING TO BE ABLE TO **JOIN** YOU FOR LUNCH AFTER **ALL**, BUT I HOPE YOU'LL HAVE **DINNER** WITH ME TONIGHT.

IT'S BEEN QUITE A **WHILE** SINCE I FOUND MYSELF FACE TO FACE WITH A BRITISH **SCHOOL KID**... I CAN'T **WAIT** TO HEAR WHAT YOU THINK OF THE **STORMBREAKER**.

THIS IS MY PERSONAL ASSISTANT, **MR GRIN**.

HE SEEMS TO HAVE **CUT** HIMSELF **SHAVING**.

MR GRIN USED TO WORK IN A **CIRCUS**. IT WAS A NOVELTY **KNIFE-THROWING** ACT. FOR A **CLIMAX**, HE CAUGHT A **SPINNING KNIFE** BETWEEN HIS **TEETH**...

...UNTIL **ONE** NIGHT, HIS MOTHER **WAVED** TO HIM FROM THE FRONT ROW AND HE MADE A **MISTAKE** WITH HIS **TIMING**.

MLRGH.

HE CAN'T **TALK**, BUT HE'LL SHOW YOU TO YOUR **ROOM** AND WE'LL MEET AGAIN **TONIGHT**. OK?

HAVE **FUN**.

BEEP

HMMM.

TIK!

SKE TECH!

YAAAAAA!

KNOCK
KNOCK

IT IS *TIME* FOR YOU TO SEE THE *STORMBREAKER*.

YOU ARE THE *FIRST* CHILD TO EXPERIENCE THE *POWER*, THE *WORLD DOMINATION* OF THE STORMBREAKER.

THIS MODEL HAS ALREADY BEEN LOADED WITH *HIGHLY DEVELOPED* PROGRAMS FOR ALL ASPECTS OF THE *SCHOOL CURRICULUM*.

SO, UM... WHERE *IS* IT?

YOU ARE *STANDING* IN IT. IT IS THE *STORMBREAKER PROTOTYPE*.

STEP ONTO THE *PLATFORM*.

DOES IT HAVE *PINBALL*?

BE *STILL*, PLEASE, WHILE WE *SCAN* YOU.

JA!
WHO **TAUGHT** YOU ABOUT COMPUTERS, KEVIN?

MY UNCLE.

HE IS A COMPUTER **WHIZ-KING**?

YOU'RE USING **SLICE-MATRIX VIRTUAL REALITY** SOFTWARE, AREN'T YOU?

NO, HE WAS A **SECURITY GUARD**. BUT HE **DIED**.

HOW DID THAT **HAPPEN**?

I DON'T **KNOW**.

BUT **ONE** DAY I'LL FIND **OUT**.

PROGRAMMING COMPLETE

MAYBE.

BUT **NOT** TODAY.

YOU WILL START WITH **SCIENCE**. PRESS **ENTER** TO BEGIN.

SCIENCE, EH? GREAT...

...**NOT**.

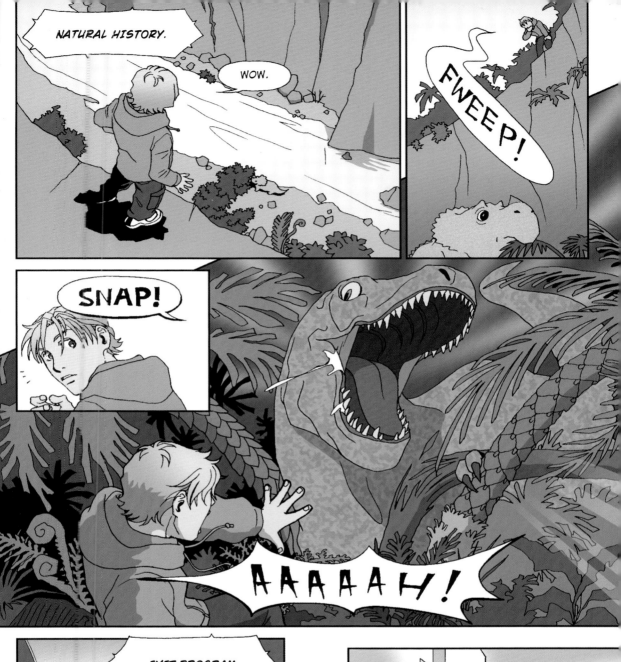

UH-OH.

GOOD **MORNING**, MR SAYLE.

IS IT **READY** FOR ME?

YES, SIR. THIS WAY, PLEASE...

!

...THE **BACKUP SYSTEM**.

IT WILL SEND OUT A **SIGNAL** THAT WILL **INSTANTLY** ACTIVATE ALL **SEVENTY THOUSAND** COMPUTERS.

OF COURSE, IT SHOULDN'T BE **NEEDED**.

NO.

IT'S **EXCELLENT**. VERY...

...GOOD.

HMMM.

KEVIN?

DIESER **VERDAMMTE** JUNGE...

HMMM.

NICE **WEATHER** FOR THE TIME OF YEAR.

HOW WOULD *YOU* KNOW? WE HAVEN'T BEEN *TOPSIDE* IN *FORTY-EIGHT HOURS*.

I'M JUST TRYING TO MAKE *CONVERSATION*.

THIRTY-NINE HOURS TO FINAL DELIVERY.

WELL, *DON'T*.

ALL BE OVER *SOON*, ANYWAY.

THIRTY-NINE HOURS AND COUNTING...

KEVIN?

WHAT ARE YOU *DOING* DOWN HERE?

MISS VOLE! I... I JUST WONDERED WHERE THIS *WENT*.

WHAT *IS* THIS PLACE?

"THIS PLACE" IS *RESTRICTED*.

BITTE, *THIS* WAY!

...

...BUT *ANYWAY.*

TELL ME, HOW DID YOU LIKE THE *STORMBREAKER?*

IT'S COOL.

"COOL." IS THAT *ALL* YOU CAN *SAY?*

YOU KNOW, KEVIN, IT STRIKES ME THAT YOU DON'T *TALK* VERY MUCH LIKE A COMPUTER *ENTHUSIAST.* NOR DO YOU *LOOK* LIKE ONE.

I'D HAVE SAID THE SAME ABOUT *YOU*, MR SAYLE.

GOOD *POINT*.

I'VE VERY MUCH *ENJOYED* MEETING YOU, KEVIN. I'M SURE YOU'LL HAVE A *LOT* TO TALK ABOUT WHEN YOU GET BACK TO *SCHOOL*.

SURE.

AND WHEN WE *LAUNCH* THE STORMBREAKERS TOMORROW...

I'LL BE THINKING *PARTICULARLY* OF YOU.

BRRRRING

CHELSEA

EXCUSE ME, FRÄULEIN.

I AM *LOOKING* FOR A PERSON CALLED *JACK*.

IS THIS ABOUT *ALEX*?

YES...

YES, IT *IS*.

THEN YOU'D BETTER COME *IN*.

YOU ARE A *FRIEND* OF ALEX?

I *LOOK AFTER* HIM.

THIS IS ALEX, YES? AND THIS *MAN* WITH HIM ... HIS *FATHER*?

HIS *UNCLE!* LOOK, WHAT'S THIS *ABOUT?*

TELL ME...

WHO *IS* THIS BOY *ALEX RIDER?* WHAT IS HE *DOING?*

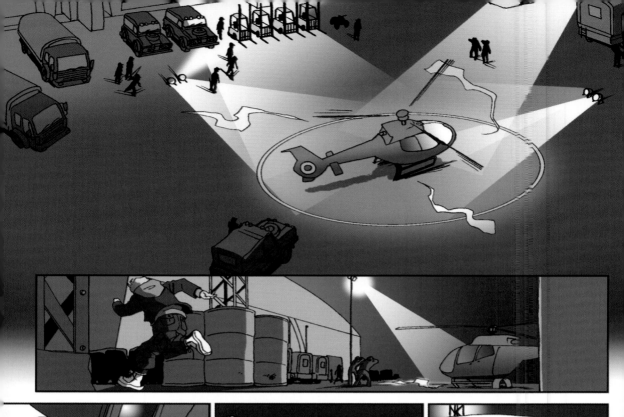

MR GREGOROVITCH!

LET US **START**.

I'M GLAD YOU WERE ABLE TO **JOIN** US TONIGHT.

I DIDN'T **REALIZE** YOU WERE GOING TO COME **PERSONALLY**.

THIS IS THE *LAST BATCH*. MY PEOPLE WANTED TO BE *ASSURED* THAT THE OPERATION HAD ALL GONE ACCORDING TO *PLAN*.

MY PLAN. *MY* OPERATION.

WHY SHOULD *YOUR* PEOPLE THINK THAT ANYTHING MIGHT GO...

KRUMP

...WRONG?

R-5

IT IS *ALL RIGHT*. THE CONTAINER IS NOT COMPROMISED.

CARRY ON!

I TOLD YOU I **DIDN'T** WANT TO BE **INTERRUPTED**–

UNLESS IT WAS **IMPORTANT**.

AND **IS** IT?

WE JUST GOT **THIS** FROM ALEX RIDER.

"GREGOROVICH"? **YASSEN** GREGOROVICH?

IT **HAS** TO BE.

I THOUGHT HE WAS STILL IN **NORTH KOREA**.

IT SEEMS **NOT**.

THIS IS THE **PROOF** YOU NEED, ALAN. THE STORMBREAKER **LAUNCH** IS LESS THAN **24 HOURS** AWAY. **CANCEL** IT.

YES. YOU'RE **RIGHT**.

I'LL PUT A **CALL** INTO **DOWNING STREET**.

AND GET ALEX **OUT**.

HE'LL BE **FLYING** OUT AT TWELVE O'CLOCK TOMORROW **ANYWAY**. NO POINT MAKING SAYLE – OR **GREGOROVICH**, COME TO THAT – **SUSPICIOUS**.

YOU CAN **MEET** HIM IF YOU LIKE. TAKE HIM OUT FOR AN **ICE CREAM**.

WHAT?

HE'S DONE VERY **WELL**. HE DESERVES A **TREAT**.

CORNWALL

SNAP.

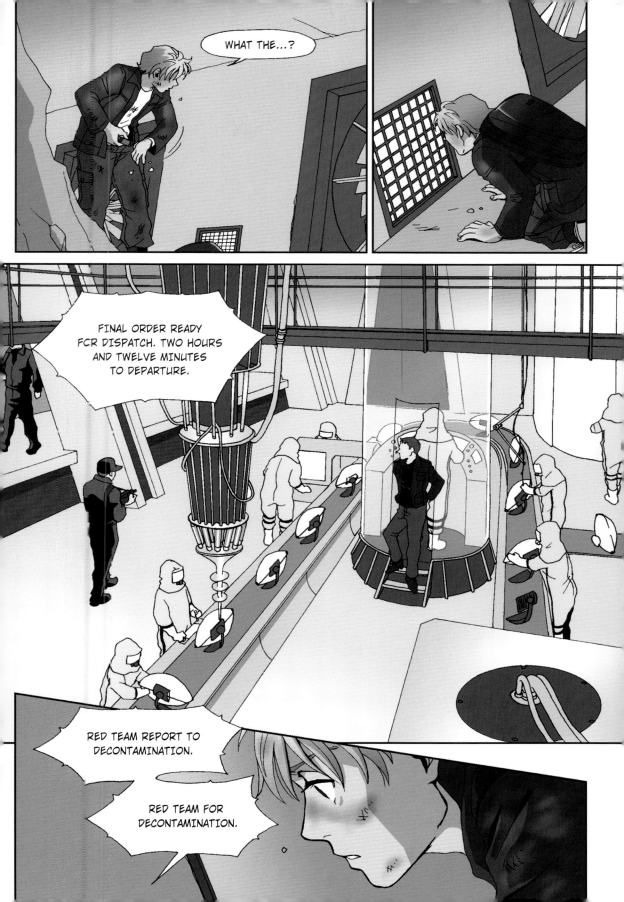

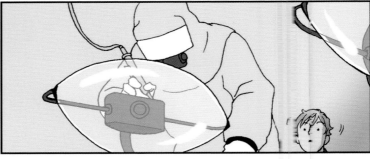

WHAT ARE YOU **DOING** HERE? WHO **ARE** YOU?

WHAT'S GOING **ON?** MY NAME'S **KEVIN BLAKE**... I WAS **INVITED** HERE.

IT IS A **GOOD ACT**. YOU DO IT VERY **WELL**. BUT YOU **SHOULDN'T** HAVE COME HERE.

WE CAN **TALK** ABOUT THIS...

I DO NOT **THINK** SO.

YES, WE **CAN!**

BE **CAREFUL!**

DO **NOT** DROP THAT...

"R5". WHAT IS IT?

PUT IT **BACK**, "KEVIN".

ALL RIGHT, THEN... WHAT'S THE WAY **OUT** OF HERE?

UP THERE.

THANKS.

CATCH!

!

BRAKKA

BRAKKA

SPTANG

BRAKKA

STOP!
STOP!

SPTANG

YOU *IDIOT!*
YOU MUST NOT
FIRE *BULLETS*
IN HERE!

OH!

OF COURSE,
I'M *SORRY.* I
WON'T DO THAT...

..AGAIN?

NO. YOU
WILL *NOT.*

SLAM!

! THERE HE IS!

BRAKKA

BRAKKA

BRAKKA

LOOK OUT!
HE'S GOT A...

...NINTENDO?

BOOM!

THUNK

IF *THIS* IS HOW YOU TREAT THE *WINNER*, I'D *HATE* TO SEE WHAT HAPPENED TO THE *RUNNER-UP*.

YOU'RE *NOT* KEVIN BLAKE.

YOU'RE *ALEX RIDER*.

YOUR *UNCLE* WAS PRETENDING TO BE A *SECURITY* GUARD, BUT *YASSEN GREGOROVICH* DEALT WITH *HIM*...

...AND *MI6* SENT *YOU* TO TAKE HIS PLACE.

SENDING A *FOURTEEN-YEAR-OLD* TO DO THEIR *DIRTY WORK*. NOT VERY *BRITISH*, I'D HAVE SAID. NOT *CRICKET*.

WHAT ARE YOU *DOING* HERE? WE *KNOW* YOU'RE PUTTING SOME KIND OF *VIRUS* INTO THE STORMBREAKER...

OH! IT'S... IT'S NOT A *COMPUTER* VIRUS, IS IT?

IT'S *THE REAL THING!*

VERY *CLEVER*, ALEX.

IT'S CALLED *R5*... A *GENETICALLY MODIFIED* VIRUS.

IT'S *VERY* NASTY.

BUT YOU'LL KILL **THOUSANDS** OF **PEOPLE!**

WHAT?

NO, NO, DON'T BE **SILLY.**

I'LL KILL **MILLIONS** OF THEM.

ALL BECAUSE YOU WERE **BULLIED** AT **SCHOOL?**

LOTS OF PEOPLE ARE BULLIED AT SCHOOL, BUT IT DOESN'T TURN **THEM** INTO **RAVING PSYCHOPATHS!**

THUNK

TIME TO SAY **GOODBYE**, ALEX.

AS YOU MAY HAVE SEEN, I'M **PACKING UP** AND **LEAVING.** I'D **LOVE** TO STAY, BUT I HAVE A RATHER IMPORTANT APPOINTMENT IN **LONDON.**

SO I'LL LEAVE YOU TO **NADIA.**

THAT WAS... A GOOD **SHOT.**

EURGH.

ACTUALLY, IT WAS A **NEAR MISS.** YOU SHOULD WATCH YOUR **MOUTH.**

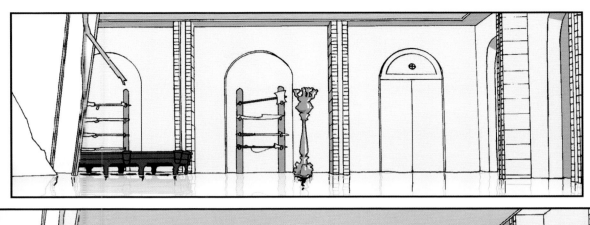

PLEEEH!

HAH

HAH

EW.

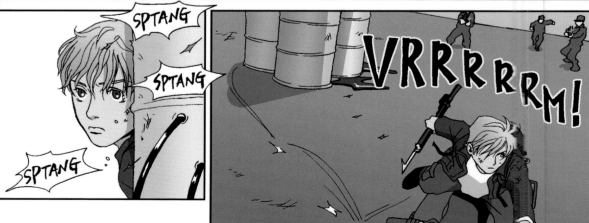

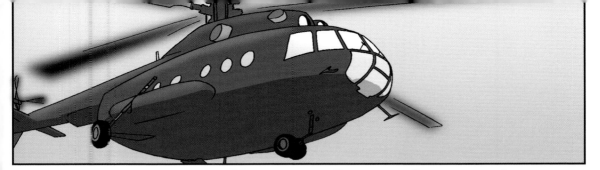

NUUUH...

EUUGH!

ALL RIGHT, MR GRIN.

I WANT YOU TO FLY ME TO *LONDON*. AS *FAST* AS YOU CAN.

YARGH...

HYDE PARK, LONDON

WE DON'T KNOW.

WHAT DO YOU *MEAN*, YOU *DON'T KNOW*? YOU *PROMISED* ME YOU'D LOOK AFTER HIM!

WE DON'T HAVE *TIME* FOR THIS NOW, MISS STARBRIGHT.

THE *PRIME MINISTER* IS...

CLAP

CLAP

CLAP

CLAP

LADIES AND GENTLEMEN, *THANK YOU*.

THE MESSAGE TODAY IS QUITE *CLEAR*.

"AND THAT MESSAGE IS *EDUCATION*. EDUCATION, EDUCATION,

AND..."

AND...

UM...

...AND *EDUCATION!*

AND *THAT* IS WHY I AM *DELIGHTED* TO ACCEPT THE *GENEROUS* OFFER MADE BY ONE OF OUR *FOREMOST ENTREPRENEURS*, AND *MY* OLD SCHOOL COLLEAGUE...

DARRIUS SMELL.

SAYLE!

DARRIUS *SAYLE!*

I WANT YOU TO KEEP FLYING *NORTH* UNTIL YOU RUN OUT OF *FUEL.* THEN YOU CAN *LAND,* OK?

NORGH.

BROOKLAND SCHOOL

YOU CAN LEAVE HIM TO *US*. DON'T *WORRY* ABOUT HIM.

YOU'VE DONE VERY *WELL*, ALEX. BUT YOU SHOULD *GO*, NOW.

WHAT ABOUT *SAYLE*?

...FINE.

HOW COULD THEY LET HIM SLIP *AWAY*?

IT'S NOT YOUR *PROBLEM*. I CAN'T BELIEVE I *EVER* LET YOU GET *MIXED UP* IN ALL THIS.

BUT IT'S *OVER* NOW, AND IT'S TIME YOU CAME *HOME*.

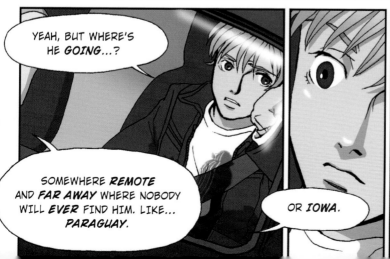

YEAH, BUT WHERE'S HE *GOING*...?

SOMEWHERE *REMOTE* AND *FAR AWAY* WHERE NOBODY WILL *EVER* FIND HIM. LIKE... *PARAGUAY*.

OR *IOWA*.

JACK! STOP THE *CAR!*

THAT'S IT!

SAYLE TOWER!

WHAT?

HE HAD A *MODEL* OF IT IN CORNWALL. HE WAS TALKING ABOUT A *BACKUP*, SOMETHING ABOUT A *MANUAL OVERRIDE*... THAT'S WHERE IT *IS*, AND THAT'S WHERE *HE* IS!

HE'S GOING TO SET OFF THE VIRUS *HIMSELF*!

COME *ON*, PUT YOUR *FOOT* DOWN!

I *CAN'T*!

WHY *NOT*? JACK, HE'LL KILL *EVERYONE*!

BECAUSE, ALEX, YOU'RE NOT IN *CORNWALL* ANY MORE.

WELCOME TO *LONDON TRAFFIC*.

NO...

THAT'S RIGHT, **MRS JONES!**

I DON'T **KNOW** WHAT HER **FIRST NAME** IS! I'M NOT SENDING HER A **BIRTHDAY** CARD, THIS IS **URGENT!** STOP MAKING ME...

...JUMP OVER HURDLES...

YAAAH!

ALEX...

KEEP GOING!

AAAAH!

WOOOAH!

WHAT THE-?

DAMNED *LUNATICS!*

AFTER THEM!

OH, NO...
DON'T LOOK ROUND!

WHY NOT?

TRUST ME!

SKREECH!

AAAH!

WHOOPS!
SORRY!

THANKS, SABINA!

STOP RIGHT THERE!

WAIT...!

NOT *AGAIN*...

WHUD!

!

SCHOOLBOY TRICK.

OODOWOOARRRRR

HEH.

HEH HEH HEH.

WHUMP

ALEX. I'M *SLIPPING...!*

TWANG

ALL RIGHT...

I'LL *SWING* YOU ONTO THE *BALCONY!*

NO, *DON'T!*

THE CABLE WILL *BREAK!*

I CAN *DO IT!*

SAYLE HAD BECOME AN **EMBARRASSMENT** TO THE PEOPLE I **WORK** FOR.

WHAT ABOUT **ME**?

I HAVE NO **INSTRUCTIONS** CONCERNING YOU.

THIS DOESN'T **CHANGE** ANYTHING.

YOU **KILLED** MY **UNCLE**. YOU'RE STILL MY **ENEMY**.

I HAVE **MANY** ENEMIES.

THIS **ISN'T OVER**, GREGOROVICH!

I THINK IT **IS**, ALEX. GO BACK TO **SCHOOL**.

YOU DO NOT **BELONG** TO MY WORLD, AND YOU SHOULD **FORGET** ABOUT ME.

I'LL **NEVER** FORGET YOU.

THAT IS **YOUR** CHOICE.

YOU DON'T *HAVE* TO WALK WITH ME TO *SCHOOL.*

I *JUST* WANT TO MAKE SURE YOU *GET* THERE, YOU KNOW?

BROOKLAND SCHOOL

HI, ALEX! YOUR *MUMPS* CLEARED UP, THEN?

HI!

WHAT DOES *HE* TEACH? AND HOW COME YOU NEVER MENTIONED HIM TO *ME* BEFORE...?